For my daughter, Reagan, who enjoys spooky tales, and her older brother Christian, who is terrified of them.

Contents

1. The Witch — 1
2. Camping — 4
3. Man at the Window — 8
4. The Bus — 11
5. The Grinner — 14
6. Want to Go for a Hike — 17
7. My New Friend — 19
8. When You're Alone — 23
9. The Schoolyard — 25
10. The Whining Pit — 29
11. House Sitting — 32
12. The Red Light — 34
13. Roommate — 37
14. Emily — 39
15. Have You Ever — 42
16. First Time — 44
17. Toys Will Be Toys — 46
18. The Painting — 49
19. Bunny — 52
20. Going Down — 56
21. Laughing Jack — 59
22. Mom — 63
23. Philip Clark — 64
24. Friday Night Out — 67
25. Abigail — 69
26. Hello Dolly — 72
27. Midnight — 76
28. Old Griswald — 79
29. The Babysitter — 82
30. Old Man — 85
31. The Basement — 88
32. Apparition — 91
33. Little Nun — 96
34. The Hollow Sisters — 100

Inspiration 103
Originals 104

THE WITCH

It was Halloween night. My buddy Cole and I were trick-or-treating. His older brother Jackson was chaperoning us. Our bags were about halfway full when we walked by the old Thatcher house. It was an old, rundown house with an overgrown lawn.

Jackson spoke up, "Why don't you guys go see how Old Morgana Thatcher is doing?"

We both looked at each other and said, "No way."

Jackson replied, "What's the matter? You're not scared of the old witch, are you?"

I replied, "There's no such thing as witches."

Jackson explained, "Oh no? The urban legend tells a tale that Morgana Thatcher started practicing witchcraft decades ago. Ever since then, no one has ever seen her come out of her house. They say if you go up to her house and peek in, you can see her floating."

Cole and I shrugged in disbelief. Jackson went on to call us chickens and dared us to go up to her house and peek in. Cole, who was braver than me and gave into name-calling much easier, agreed and ran up to the house. I watched as he tried to look through the windows that were all boarded up. After a minute, he came back.

"Well, what did you see?" Jackson asked.

"Nothing really. Just cobwebs and dusty furniture," Cole replied.

"See! Nothing to worry about," said Jackson. "Go on, your turn."

I paused hesitantly and decided if Cole could do it and nothing happened, so could I. My heart raced as I stumbled up the creaking stairs to the crumbling house. *Everything is fine. There's no such thing as witches*, I thought to myself, trying to remain calm.

Taking a deep breath, I inched forward. I was glad my back was to my friends, so they couldn't see how scared I was. I carefully stepped forward and squinted into the dust-covered window. The house was almost pitch-black. I couldn't see anything.

I moved closer to the door and noticed it was a really old-fashioned kind with a large keyhole. I bent down and looked through. All I could see was bright white, like something was blocking the other side. I stood up and walked back to the guys.

As we walked away from the house, Jackson remembered another part of the legend of Morgana Thatcher.

"They say to never let Morgana catch you looking at her. If you ever look into her eyes, she will haunt you forever… Those creepy bright white eyes," Jackson said.

I replied in a trembling voice, "Did you say, WHITE?"

CAMPING

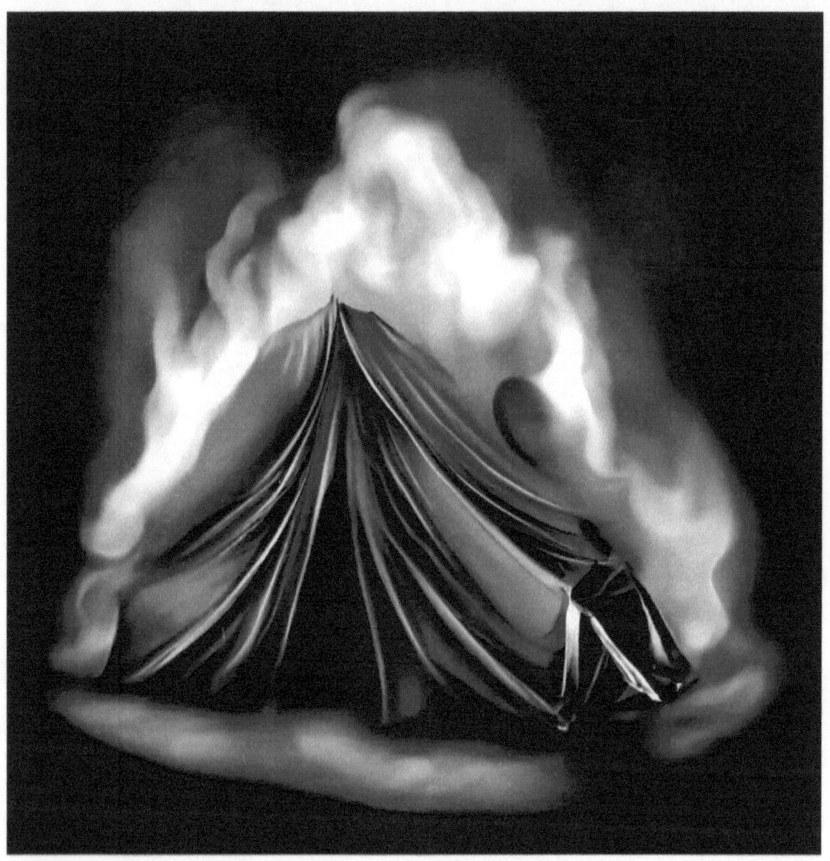

Once upon a moonlit night, two adventurous best friends, Alex and Jake, decided to embark on a camping trip in the deep, mysterious woods near their small town. Armed with their trusty tent, sleeping bags, and a sense of excitement, they set up camp beneath the towering trees.

As the night settled in, the boys sat by the campfire, sharing stories and laughter, oblivious to the eerie silence that surrounded them.

"Hey, remember that time we went hiking in the mountains?" Jake asked, a hint of nostalgia in his voice.

Alex chuckled, stirring the fire with a stick. "Oh yeah, the one where you almost tripped over that snake?"

Their laughter echoed through the forest, but it was short-lived. As the embers dimmed, they began to notice subtle, unnerving sounds in the darkness.

"Did you hear that?" whispered Jake, his eyes darting around.

Alex, who had been listening intently, replied, "Yeah, it sounds like footsteps, but there's no one else out here, right?"

Footsteps seemed to circle their tent as if someone or something was prowling just beyond the thin fabric. The joyful atmosphere from moments ago had shifted into a tense silence.

Nervous giggling and whispers, like the laughter of children, floated through the air. The boys exchanged puzzled glances, wondering who could be playing tricks on them in the heart of the woods. Alex attempted to dismiss it as just their imagination, but Jake couldn't shake the feeling that something wasn't right.

In the middle of the night, when the darkness was at its peak, they heard a thud against the side of their tent. They could see what looked like hands pressing against the side of the tent wall. Heartbeats thundering in their ears, they cautiously peered outside, using a small hole in the tent's opening. What they saw made their hair stand on end: ghostly figures, like pale shadows, darting between the trees, giggling and hiding as if playing a haunting game of hide-and-seek.

Fear gripped their hearts, but curiosity pushed them to keep observing. Suddenly, the temperature inside the tent plummeted, creating frosty clouds with every breath they took. They huddled together for warmth, seeking comfort in their friendship as the ghostly figures continued to move silently through the woods.

Then, as if on cue, the forest fell silent. No more footsteps, whispers, or giggles reached their ears. The woods seemed to hold its breath, and even the nocturnal creatures were hushed. The boys exchanged glances, anxiety now dancing in their eyes. They knew something was about to happen, but they couldn't fathom what.

Time dragged on, and despite the silence, they felt an ominous presence surrounding them. The eerie stillness made their skin crawl, and they couldn't shake the feeling of being watched by unseen eyes.

Morning eventually arrived, bringing with it a mixture of relief and apprehension. The boys emerged from their tent, the first rays of dawn revealing a seemingly normal forest, absent of any ghosts or mysterious figures.

As they packed up their campsite, Alex and Jake exchanged words of confusion and disbelief, questioning the reality of their chilling encounter.

Alex furrowed his brow, folding up a tent flap, and said, "I can't stop thinking about what happened last night, Jake. It was like something was messing with us."

Jake, his eyes still darting around the forest, responded, "I know, man. It felt so surreal. Do you think it could've been animals or the light playing tricks with our eyes?"

Alex paused, pondering the question, then replied, "I wish. But I really don't think so."

As they finished packing up their gear, their eyes caught a glimpse of something that froze them both in fear. They could see tiny footprints, the size of little children, in the dirt all around their campsite. Jake and Alex both said to each other, with fear in their voices, "Let's get out of here."

From that day on, the two boys never ventured into those woods again. They could never forget the Unexplainable events that had unfolded under the moon's spooky glow. Whether it was just a vivid imagination or a true brush with the supernatural, they had learned a valuable lesson: some mysteries are better left untouched, and the secrets of the woods should remain hidden in the shadows of the night.

MAN AT THE WINDOW

My neighbor across the street has always given me an uneasy feeling. There was just something about him that creeped me out.

One night, my parents were out at a dinner party while I stayed home to watch some TV. Being alone, I always liked to keep the lights in the house off. I didn't like the idea that someone outside could see me if I had the lights on.

As I was settling down to watch my TV show, I heard someone banging on the front door. The sound of a door knocking when I am alone in the house always frightened me. With a sudden jolt, my heart began racing. I didn't want to answer it, scared of what might be on the other side. Finally, the knocking stopped.

I went back to watching my TV show. Just then, I heard the knocking at the door, this time even louder, more frantic. Frozen in fear again, I waited until the knocking stopped. Not more than a few seconds later, I saw a man in the window, knocking and yelling. As I looked at the window, I could finally see that it was my neighbor. He was knocking, screaming, and pointing at me with a wide-eyed, frightening face. He flashed a flashlight through the window, searching for me since the lights were off.

I finally came to my senses and screamed at my neighbor, "Go away or I'll call the cops." His flashlight, still searching for me through the window. He must have heeded my warning because moments later he left the window.

My relief didn't last long, as I saw my neighbor in a different window. Banging and yelling, flashlight piercing through the window again.

I had enough. I was so scared that I picked up the phone and called 911 and let them know that someone was trying to break into my house.

I was lucky enough that the police arrived so quickly. I watched as they started arresting my neighbor. I opened the door to see them in person. That's when I heard my neighbor frantically telling the police, "I am not trying to break in. I was trying to warn her about the other man that broke into her house."

My heart sank, my body frozen solid with such terror. A police officer ran towards me and went into the house just as a man in a black hoodie burst through the backdoor. "Oh my God! That man was in my house!" I said to myself. The police officer chased after the man and ended up catching him a block away.

The first banging on my door was the man trying to break in. My neighbor had seen him from across the street, breaking in through a side window. My neighbor ran over to try and warn me about the man. I am forever grateful for my neighbor whom I had once thought to be creepy. If it weren't for him, I don't know what might have happened.

THE BUS

In the quiet, very small town of Grimshire, there existed a chilling legend that sent shivers down the spines of schoolchildren. It was said that on certain afternoons when a child was all alone waiting for the bus, an eerie specter would appear—the ghostly school bus.

The tale was whispered among students, a secret they shared

with hushed excitement. Some claimed to have seen it—a decrepit yellow bus, its paint peeling and windows cracked, rolling silently to a stop where the children gathered. They spoke of mist swirling around the bus, giving it an otherworldly aura.

One fateful afternoon, as the school bell rang, signaling the end of the day, a young boy named Tim found himself alone at the bus loop, waiting for his bus to arrive to take him home. He watched as the other students climbed into their familiar cars and buses, leaving him in the gathering dusk. Anxiety prickled at his skin, and he couldn't shake off the eerie feeling that he was being watched.

And then, it appeared—the ghostly school bus. Tim's heart quickened, his breath catching in his throat. It seemed to glide effortlessly to a halt, its doors creaking open as if beckoning him inside. Uncertain but desperate not to be left behind, Tim hesitantly stepped on board. There was a force luring him inside as if he couldn't control it.

The interior of the bus was icy cold, and a thick fog hung in the air, obscuring his view. He stumbled down the aisle to find a seat. As he settled his seat, a cold breeze caressed his neck, chilling him to the bone. He turned his gaze toward the front of the bus, and his blood ran cold.

The figure behind the wheel was no ordinary bus driver—it was a ghastly apparition, its face pale and mottled, eyes hollow and lifeless. Its twisted smile sent a wave of terror crashing over Tim, freezing him in place. He realized with dread that he had unwittingly boarded a bus driven by a specter from the other side.

The bus pulled away from the curb, gliding through the town's streets with an otherworldly silence. Shadows danced on the windows, casting eerie shapes that seemed to taunt Tim from the darkness outside. The bus driver's haunting laughter filled the air, chilling his very soul.

As the bus journeyed deeper into the night, Tim's fear intensified. He tried to scream for help, but his voice was swallowed by the oppressive atmosphere. The ghostly passengers around him stared forward, their eyes empty voids, as if they were trapped in an eternal purgatory.

Time seemed to stretch endlessly until, with a sudden jolt, the bus screeched to a halt. Tim's heart pounded in his chest as the doors swung open. The bus driver turned toward him, its voice a haunting whisper that echoed through his mind.

"You have ventured into the realm of the lost, child," the ghastly figure hissed. "You belong with us now."

Then, the bus driver let out a loud sinister laugh.

In a moment of sheer terror, Tim broke free from the paralyzing grip of fear. He stumbled toward the exit, throwing himself into the unknown darkness beyond. The bus disappeared into thin air, leaving Tim alone on the deserted road near his house, gasping for breath.

Tim's encounter with the ghostly school bus would forever haunt him. From that day forward, he warned others, sharing his tale of the ghastly bus and its spectral driver. And so, the legend grew stronger, serving as a chilling reminder to the children of Grimshire never to board the ghostly school bus.

THE GRINNER

Once upon a time, in a quiet town, there lived a young girl named Hannah. She was known for her vibrant personality and kind heart. However, her life took a sinister turn when she started experiencing something inexplicably terrifying.

It all began on a cloudy evening when Hannah was walking home from her friend's house. As she made her way down the road along the woods, she caught a glimpse of a figure lurking in the shadows. Intrigued and slightly unnerved, she turned to get a better look, only to see a pair of piercing, glowing eyes staring back at her.

The figure wore a tattered cloak that concealed its body, leaving only its head visible. Its head, framed by long, thin strands of hair, bore a malevolent appearance with a ghastly grin on its pale face. Its grin seemed to stretch impossibly wide, displaying rows of sharp, jagged teeth. From that moment on, Hannah became haunted by the relentless presence of the grinning figure.

No matter where Hannah went, the figure followed, always lurking just beyond her sight. It appeared in her peripheral vision, just around corners, or peering out from behind trees. Its sinister grin chilled Hannah to the bone, evoking a sense of dread that seemed to seep into her very soul.

Hannah confided in her friends and family, desperately seeking answers or a way to rid herself of this haunting figure. They tried to dismiss it as a figment of her imagination or a trick of the shadows, but Hannah knew better. The figure was real, and its relentless pursuit grew more intense with each passing day.

Sleep became a torment for Hannah, for even in her dreams, the grinning figure appeared. Its laughter echoed through her mind, an eerie symphony that shattered her sense of safety. Hannah's once vibrant spirit started to wither, her once-joyful demeanor replaced by a constant state of anxiety.

As time went on, Hannah's fear began to consume her. The grinning figure had become an ever-present shadow, a reminder of her vulnerability and the uncertainty that shrouded her life.

And then, one night, as Hannah lay awake in her bed, she heard a soft tapping at her window. Trembling with fear, she approached and cautiously pulled back the curtains. There, perched on the windowsill, was the grinning figure, its eyes fixed on her.

A chilling gust of wind swept through the room, extinguishing the night light on the wall, and plunging Hannah into darkness. She could sense the figure's presence drawing closer, its cold breath against her cheek. Panic consumed her, and she screamed for help.

When her family rushed into her room, they found Hannah trembling and tears streaming down her face. But to their shock, there was no trace of the grinning figure. It had vanished, leaving only an air of evil behind.

Days turned into weeks, and the figure did not reappear. Hannah slowly regained a semblance of her former self, but the memory of the grinning figure never faded.

To this day, the mystery of the grinning figure remains unsolved. Was it a ghost, a demon, or something even more sinister? No one can say for certain. But every now and then, on a moonlit night when the world is silent, some claim to see a fleeting glimpse of a figure with a terrifying grin.

Want to Go for a Hike

My girlfriend Holly and I went on an 8-day hiking trip. We went through the Appalachian Trail where it was just us and no people for miles in each direction. We both love the outdoors, and she especially enjoys photographing nature. She brought her expensive digital camera and spent hours taking pictures every day. She must have taken thousands of photos. Photos of birds, animals on the ground, streams we passed by, and even some goofy ones of myself.

Each night, we would have a small fire and then sleep in our small tent. After our trip, we returned home. By the time we got home, it was really late, so we quickly ate and went to bed.

The next day, Holly connected her camera to the computer to start looking through all the photos she had taken. A few hundred photos in, which would be around the 2nd day of our trip, she noticed photos of us. Us sleeping in our tent. This really freaked us out because we didn't take these photos, and we were miles away from anyone.

As she looked through more photos, on about the 4th day, we saw more pictures of us sleeping in the tent. We were terrified at this point. Who was taking her camera and photographing us while we slept?

Then, our hearts sank in absolute horror. At the very end of the photos, we saw pictures of us again. But these were different. It wasn't us in our tent. It was us sleeping in our bed.

My New Friend

A young boy named Christian had just moved into town with his family, seeking friendship and adventure in his unfamiliar surroundings.

Christian walked to the local convenience store. As Christian entered the store, his arrival immediately caught the attention of a peculiar boy named Branson—a mischievous boy with an alluring charm. Branson was quick to approach Christian, offering companionship and a promise of thrilling adventures. Eager to make friends, Christian gladly accepted Branson's invitation to play. Christian said, "I have to bring these groceries home first and have dinner. Then, I can ask my mom if we can play after that."

Branson replied, "Great! Meet me at the park by the edge of the woods right over there. I have something really cool to show you."

Christian looked as Branson pointed across the street to an open clearing with some woods on the edge. "Okay. I will see you there," Christian responded.

That evening, Branson led Christian through winding paths and twisted branches, eventually arriving at the edge of the town's oldest cemetery. The moon's pale glow cast an eerie light upon the tombstones, lending an otherworldly atmosphere to the scene.

"Let's play a game of hide and seek," Branson proposed excitedly. "But in the dark, where the real fun lies."

Christian hesitated, his heart fluttering with a mix of excitement and unease. Against his better judgment, he agreed, his desire for acceptance overriding his instincts. Branson's eyes glinted with mischief as he counted to ten, while Christian rushed to find a hiding spot among the silent gravestones.

As Christian darted between the tombstones, the air grew thick with a chilling breeze. Shadows danced and twisted, their grotesque shapes taunting him as he searched for the perfect hiding spot. Panic clutched at his chest, but he pressed on, determined to outwit his new friend.

Finding what he thought was the perfect hiding spot behind a weathered gravestone, Christian froze. The moon's glow revealed the name etched upon it—a name that struck him with paralyzing terror. It was Branson's grave.

A chill raced down Christian's spine, his breath catching in his throat. The realization crashed upon him like a wave—the friend he thought he was playing with was a restless spirit.

Branson's voice seeped through the night. The voice of Branson echoed in Christian's ears, distorted and filled with an otherworldly despair. "Ready or not, here I come, Christian."

With trembling limbs, Christian sprinted through the maze of tombstones, the ground seeming to shift beneath him. He dared not look back, fearing the ghostly figure of his newfound friend would chase him relentlessly.

As he burst through the cemetery gates, the moonlight bathed him in a warm embrace, relieving him of the ghostly presence. Christian collapsed onto the ground, gasping for breath, his heart pounding with the realization that he had narrowly escaped the clutches of a ghostly spirit.

The next day, Christian raced back to the convenience store. He walked up to the cashier and asked, "Do you remember the boy that was with me here yesterday?"

The cashier responded, "I don't recall seeing you with anyone yesterday. In fact, I remember talking to my co-worker about you, saying how peculiar it was that you seemed to be talking to yourself."

Christian, now confused, said, "Okay. Thanks." He started walking out of the store when out of the corner of his eye he spotted a picture of Branson on the wall. He ran over and started to read the newspaper clipping. *Boy Mysteriously Found Dead: Branson Allen.* Christian ran back to the cashier and said, "That's him! That's the boy I was in here with yesterday."

The cashier with a frightened sad look on his face explained, "That boy was found dead 7 years ago. They say he was supposed to meet some friends to play hide and seek one evening and he didn't come home that night. They found him a few days later."

Christian just stood there in shock. He didn't know what to

think. He left the store and started walking home, passing by the woods where he had escaped the night before. He couldn't help but think to himself, "If I hadn't escaped, would that have happened to me too?"

From that day on, Christian kept the memory of Branson's grave etched in his mind, a reminder of the darkness that lurks beneath seemingly innocent friendships.

WHEN YOU'RE ALONE

Have you ever wondered how the scariest things to you aren't real things? It's the supernatural and unknown things that your imagination creates. It's not a bear or even a vampire that is coming for you. It's that moment when you feel truly alone.

You lay there in your bed in complete silence, your imagination running wild. You stare around your room, wondering, "Is there something in here with me? Did I just hear a noise? Is that shadow something or someone? Is that something in the corner?" Your heart is now racing as you tremble in fear of the unknown.

Out of the corner of your eye, you see your closet door open an inch. You think to yourself, "Didn't I close it all the way?" You keep staring at it, willing it away. "Is something in there looking out at me? Should I get up and close it so I can stop thinking about it?"

But then you remember, you haven't looked in the corner in a while. And, Oh my god! What if something is under the bed? You can't get up now, or it might grab you. Now you are trapped all night, stuck with your imagination of horror.

Sleep tight.

THE SCHOOLYARD

In a small town nestled between eerie woods and misty hills, there stood an old schoolyard that had been abandoned for decades. Legend has it that the school had been closed due to a series of unexplainable tragedies and mysterious disappearances. The locals whispered tales of an evil presence that haunted the playground.

A group of adventurous kids, led by their bold and curious friend named Alex, heard these haunting tales, and became fascinated by the haunted schoolyard. One summer evening, as the sun began to set, they gathered at the edge of the woods, their hearts pounding with excitement.

Among the group was Lily, whose parents had strictly forbidden her from going anywhere near the schoolyard. They had heard the stories too, and Lily's mother warned her about the evil that dwelled there. However, the allure of the forbidden and the thrill of a ghostly adventure were too strong for the kids to resist.

With flashlights in hand and nerves of steel, they ventured into the abandoned playground. As they crossed the threshold, a chilling wind seemed to sweep through the air, causing the trees to sway ominously. Alex pressed forward, leading the way with determination, while the others followed hesitantly, their breaths visible in the cold night.

The moment they stepped onto the grounds, an invisible force seemed to tug at their clothes, pulling them backward. Fear crept into their minds, but they dismissed it as their imagination running wild. They continued deeper into the heart of the schoolyard, guided by the distant sound of eerie children's laughter echoing through the stillness.

The laughter grew louder and more menacing with each step they took. They exchanged nervous glances but urged each other on, not wanting to be the first to back out. The playground that once held joy and laughter was now filled with an unsettling darkness that clung to every corner.

As they approached the decaying school building, they saw a ghostly figure standing by the swing set, a young girl with a sad smile on her face. Her eyes were hollow and filled with sorrow as she stared at them. She spoke in a hushed whisper, "Leave this place, for it is not meant for the living."

The children hesitated, their bravery waning, but Alex, fueled by curiosity, stepped forward and asked, "Who are you? What happened here?"

The ghostly girl's voice trembled as she recounted the tragedy that had befallen her and the other children. Many years ago, the school had been a happy place until an evil spirit took hold of the schoolyard. It fed on the children's fear and despair, it triggered a sequence of terrifying events that resulted in the disappearance of several children and eventually led to the closure of the school.

She warned the kids that the evil spirit still roamed these grounds, seeking to trap the living souls within its grasp. "Leave before it's too late," she pleaded.

Fear and concern etched on their faces, the kids debated whether to heed the ghostly girl's warning or press on with their adventure. But as they looked into each other's eyes, they knew it was time to leave. The darkness was too much to bear, and they didn't want to meet the same fate as those who had come before.

They turned away from the ghostly girl and ran back toward their homes, their hearts pounding with terror. The invisible force seemed to push them harder, urging them to leave as quickly as possible.

As they walked away, an unseen force grabbed Lily by her ankles, making her fall to the ground. The invisible force dragged her towards the school building. Alex's heart now pounding in fear. He ran after Lily and grabbed her by the hands, pulling her backward with all his might. It didn't help. The force was too strong. It was now dragging Alex too.

The rest of the group was too afraid to help and stood there in shock. As Alex and Lily were dragged closer and closer to the school building, eyes filled with frightened tears, a figure appeared next to them. It was the girl. All of a sudden, the force that was pulling on them stopped. The girl urged them, "Hurry! Get out of here now. I can't stop it for long."

Alex helped Lily up and they both ran towards the group of friends, still frozen in fear. "C'mon, let's go," Alex screamed at the group. They all ran away from the school and towards the woods.

Once they crossed the threshold back into the safety of the woods, the haunting laughter and heavy atmosphere dissipated, leaving only the memory of their chilling encounter.

THE WHINING PIT

There once was a young girl named Reagan. She was known for her constant whining and complaining about every little thing. She would whine about being bored and having nothing to do. She would whine about wanting everything she saw at the store. No matter the situation, her voice carried the piercing sound of dissatisfaction. Her parents, growing weary of her constant complaints, often warned her about the consequences of her behavior.

Reagan's father, in particular, would sternly caution her, saying, "You better stop whining, Reagan, or the demons will come up out of the ground and take you away." But Reagan, a stubborn child, dismissed her father's warnings as mere tales meant to scare her into silence.

As days turned into weeks, Reagan's whining only grew louder and more relentless. Her parents' pleas for her to change her ways fell upon deaf ears. One night, after another day of incessant complaints, Reagan retreated to her bedroom.

As she lay on her bed, her whining still echoing in the air, an ominous change began to stir beneath her feet. The ground beneath Reagan's room trembled as if something restless was awakening from a deep slumber. A bright orange glow seeped through the cracks in the floor, casting an eerie light that danced across the walls.

Reagan, startled but still skeptical, gazed in disbelief as the glow intensified, illuminating her room with an otherworldly brilliance. The ground beneath her bed split open, revealing a deep, gaping pit. The room was filled with an awful stench and eerie voices not of this world.

With a horrifying realization, Reagan watched as tiny, twisted figures emerged from the pit. They were the demons her father had warned her about, their malevolent eyes glowing with an unholy light. These wicked creatures surrounded Reagan, their laughter mingling with her whines, their clawed hands reaching out to claim her.

As they closed in, Reagan's screams filled the air, but it was too late. The demons, fueled by her whining, seized her, and dragged her down into the pit, vanishing from sight. The pit closed behind them, leaving no trace of the girl who had once filled the air with her discontent.

Reagan's parents, devastated by the loss of their daughter, were left to bear the burden of their warnings gone unheeded. They grieved for the girl who had been consumed by her own negativity, forever lost to the clutches of the underworld.

HOUSE SITTING

My aunt and uncle live in a really big house on the lake. They have 2.5 acres of land. They were taking a trip to go skiing and asked if I could house-sit for them. I always wanted to live in a mansion, and this was going to be awesome.

I arrived at their house, and they showed me all around. The house had 5 bedrooms and 6 bathrooms. The kitchen was almost as big as my parents' first floor. There was a giant balcony on the 2nd floor and a huge wrap-around porch around the whole house. They said I could eat whatever I wanted from the fridge. After saying our goodbyes, I decided to walk around the property and enjoy the sunny day by the lake.

Once it got close to dinner time, I went back inside to get something to eat. I sat at the table and had some leftover lasagna my aunt had made. Just then, I felt a breeze from behind me. The door was open. I must not have shut it all the way.

After that, I went into my aunt and uncle's bedroom to watch some TV. They said I could if I wanted to because their room has this amazing projector screen that feels like a huge movie theater. As I was watching my show, I noticed a figure in the corner of the room. There was a statue of a mime just looking at me. It looked exactly like that famous mime, Marcel Marceau. It had an all-white face, arched eyebrows, and black lips with a wide grin.

As I kept watching TV, I kept having this uneasy feeling like the mime statue was watching me. Its eyes looked so real. It felt like a person just standing there looking at me.

Staring at it, I decided I wasn't going to look at this thing all night. I got up and threw a comforter over it. "There, that's better." I went back to watching my show.

Moments later, I got a call from my aunt and uncle to check in on me. They asked how everything was going and if the food in the fridge was okay. I told them everything was great and that I was enjoying their awesome projector screen. I mentioned how the mime statue in the corner of their room creeped me out.

The phone went silent for a few seconds. Then I heard my uncle say in a scared, confused voice, "We don't have a mime statue."

The Red Light

In the small town of Hisle, Kentucky, there was a peculiar legend that sent shivers down the spines of children and adults alike. Rumors of a mysterious red light that appeared deep within the woods circulated through the community, igniting both curiosity and fear.

According to the stories passed down from generation to generation, the red light would manifest without warning, casting an eerie glow amidst the darkness of the night. It seemed to beckon those who caught sight of it, drawing them into the depths of the haunting forest. No one knew its origin or purpose, but the tales of those who had encountered the light painted a chilling picture.

The children of the town were especially vulnerable to the enchanting allure of the crimson glow. They would gather around campfires, sharing tales of bravery and daring while secretly hoping they would never stumble upon the mysterious light themselves. But despite their fears, a mysterious curiosity tugged at their hearts, daring them to venture into the woods in search of the mystical red light.

On moonlit nights, when the forest stood in silent anticipation, children would gather at the edge of the woods, their breaths shallow and hearts pounding. One by one, they would take hesitant steps into the darkness, their eyes darting nervously as they peered into the shadows, searching for that elusive red light.

As they delved deeper into the woods, their fear intensified. The trees seemed to close in around them, whispering eerie sounds carried by the wind. Branches brushed against their skin, making their hairs stand on end. Yet, despite the immense fear that gripped them, they pressed on, their curiosity guiding their every step.

Suddenly, through the thick foliage, a soft crimson glow pierced the darkness. The children's hearts skipped a beat, their breath caught in their throats. The red light grew brighter and pulsated, casting distorted shadows that seemed to come alive.

Hypnotized by the captivating glow, the children moved closer, their eyes fixated on the pulsating light. It seemed to whisper promises of adventure and wonder, promising a world beyond their wildest dreams. But as they approached, a chilling realization began to dawn upon them—the red light was leading them deeper into the heart of the forest, away from the safety of their homes.

Panic gripped the children, snapping them out of their trance-like state. They turned to retreat, but the path they had taken seemed to have vanished. Panic surged through their veins as they realized they were trapped, ensnared by the alluring trap of the red light.

The once-alluring glow transformed into a malevolent force, casting twisted shadows that seemed to sneer and laugh at their predicament. The children screamed for help, their cries swallowed by the suffocating darkness that surrounded them.

Legend has it that some of the children managed to escape, haunted by the memory of the red light for the rest of their lives. But others were never seen again, swallowed by the depths of the forest, forever entwined in its sinister embrace.

To this day, tales are told to the children of the town of Hisle, warning them of the treacherous allure of the red light. They are taught to stay away from the woods at night, to resist the enchanting whispers that call from within.

ROOMMATE

I have been having issues with sleeping. I just can't breathe very well. My doctor asked that I record myself sleeping so that I can hear how bad it sounds to know if I have sleep apnea. I downloaded this app on my phone for recording sounds and set the recorder to record most of the night.

I go to sleep and wake up the next day. In the morning, I pour some cereal and sit at the kitchen table. I open my recording app and start playing it. I can see the sound wave bars in the app when my sleep apnea starts getting loud. I fast-forward to that part. That's when I heard it. My bedroom door creaking open. Then, about 30 seconds later, I heard breathing. Not from me. I hear a second person breathing.

"I live alone."

EMILY

In the heart of a bustling city stood a grand old hotel. The hotel was built on the very grounds where a tragic fire had claimed the life of a young girl long ago, a secret that the world had forgotten. She was home alone when the fire took her life.

Legend spoke of a young girl named Emily, who became a restless spirit, forever seeking her lost parents. Her spirit wandered the hotel's corridors, a ghost forever yearning for the love and warmth she had lost.

Visitors to the hotel would often share chilling tales of strange occurrences. Guests reported an overwhelming scent of smoke that permeated the air, clinging to their clothes and filling their senses. People would see footprints of water leaving the hotel pool with no trace of the person who left them. Rumors circulated, suggesting that it was the lingering presence of Emily.

One stormy night, a young girl arrived at the hotel. As she settled into her room, an inexplicable chill washed over her, sending shivers down her spine. The faint aroma of smoke filled the air, and her heart quickened as she recognized it from the stories she had heard from the hotel visitors.

Night after night, the young girl became increasingly plagued by strange occurrences. She would wake to the sound of creaking floorboards outside her room, only to find nothing but darkness and silence. Unseen hands brushed against her skin, leaving a cold, lingering touch that chilled her to her core.

Driven by curiosity and a deep-seated empathy for the lost spirit, the young girl delved into the hotel's history with unwavering determination, uncovering the tragic tale of Emily and the fire that had claimed her life. Late nights were spent poring over dusty archives and faded newspaper clippings, each word a breadcrumb leading her closer to the heart-wrenching truth.

The more she learned, the stronger her connection to Emily became, as if the little girl's spirit had chosen her to be her confidante. It was as though the echoes of Emily's laughter, silenced by tragedy, resonated in her soul. She began to imagine the joyous moments that Emily had once experienced and the heart-wrenching fear she must have felt as the flames engulfed her world.

She felt an obligation to honor Emily's memory. She left no stone unturned in her quest to ensure that Emily's story was not lost to time, as she believed that in preserving the memory of this lost soul, she could bring some measure of solace to the tormented spirit that had chosen her as its guardian.

Driven by a desire to help Emily find peace, the young girl ventured into the darkest corners of the hotel, following the faint scent of smoke that led her through the maze-like hallways. She searched for clues, piecing together fragments of the past and reliving the fateful night that forever changed Emily's life.

As the young girl ventured deeper into the bowels of the hotel, she stumbled upon a hidden chamber, untouched by time. The room was filled with charred remnants, a chilling reminder of the fire that had consumed Emily's home. And there, amidst the wreckage, the young girl found Emily's old hand mirror. She held it up and saw a reflection of herself, but it was distorted, ethereal.

At that moment, realization washed over the girl. The young girl she had sought to help, the one she believed was Emily, was in fact herself. She was the restless spirit, trapped in a cycle of searching for her parents, never truly aware of her own fate.

Tears streamed down Emily's face as she accepted her tragic destiny. The fire had stolen her life, and the hotel had become her eternal purgatory. The scent of smoke that clung to her was a reminder of her demise.

With a heavy heart, Emily whispered a final farewell to the hotel and the life she had once known. Her spirit faded into the shadows as she was finally able to move on into the afterlife.

HAVE YOU EVER

Have you ever watched one of those videos where you are supposed to really focus your attention on something so that you can find the really interesting thing in the video? And then, at the end, they reveal that you were looking so hard for something that you completely didn't notice this other thing moving in the video. It's amazing how your brain doesn't pick up on that. Like, as you were reading this, I snuck into your house.

43

First Time

I am ten years old. My whole life, my parents told me never to open the basement door. I often sit and wonder, what could be on the other side of that door? I've heard whispers from my parents but could never really make out what it was. Was there a monster on the other side? Was there something so terrifying that they were protecting me from it?

One day, I decided that I had to see for myself what was on the other side. When I knew my parents had gone to the store, I grabbed a crowbar from the tool bench and walked over to the basement door. I tried prying the lock off. With all my might I pulled. I ended up breaking the hinge instead of the lock. With the door now ready to be opened, I slowly pushed on the basement door, lifting it up.

What I saw at first was so blinding. This immense light shining right into my eyes. It hurt my eyes so badly at first, but then they started to adjust. I pushed the door fully open and walked up the stairs and out of the doorway. What I saw was… Beautiful. I saw the ground covered in this hairy, amazing deep color green. I saw the giant brown pillars with more deep green coming out of the tops of them. There was a ball of light in the sky so bright, it hurt my eyes to stare at it. This was the first time I had ever seen anything like this.

Toys Will Be Toys

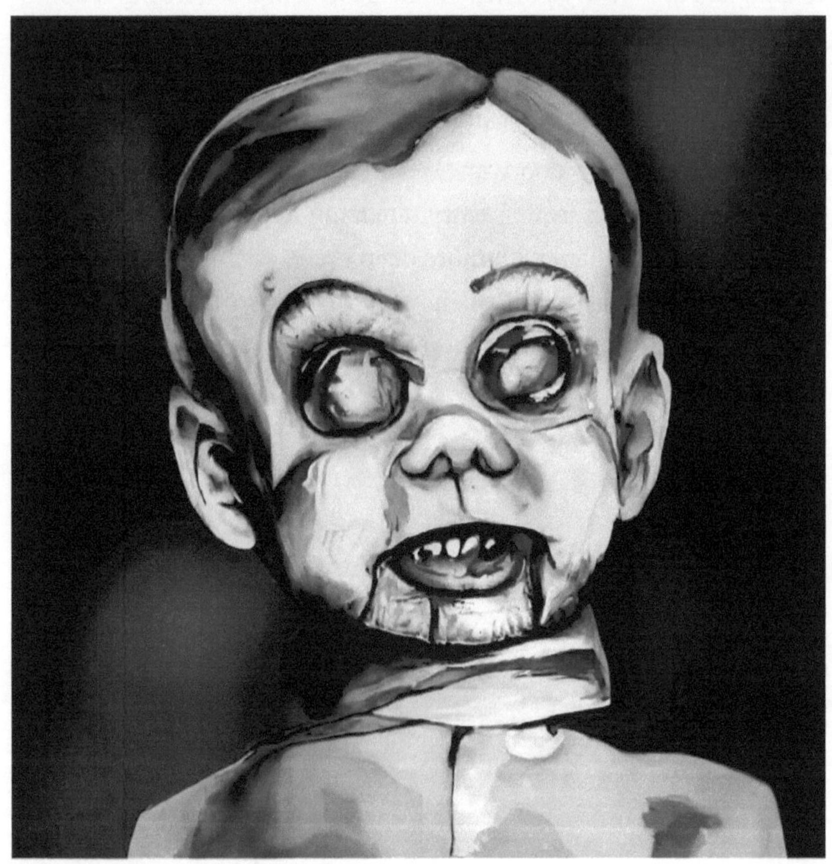

Once upon a time, in a quiet suburban neighborhood, there lived a young boy named Henry. Henry had always been fascinated by ventriloquist dummies, finding them both intriguing and a little creepy. One day, his parents surprised him with a beautifully crafted ventriloquist dummy as a birthday gift.

The dummy had glassy eyes that seemed to follow Henry's

every move and a wide, toothy grin that gave him an unsettling feeling. Its name was Mr. Chuckles, and it quickly became Henry's favorite toy. Henry would spend hours practicing his ventriloquism skills, creating lively conversations between himself and Mr. Chuckles.

However, as Henry spent more time with the dummy, strange things began to happen. Henry would wake up in the middle of the night to find Mr. Chuckles sitting at the foot of his bed, his lifeless eyes fixed on him. The room would grow cold, and Henry could swear he heard whispers as if the dummy were speaking to him when he was alone.

As the days went by, Henry's other toys seemed to come alive as well. He would find them in unexpected places, their positions shifting as if they had been moved by invisible forces. He would hear faint giggles and tiny footsteps in his room, even when he knew he was alone.

Terrified, Henry confided in his parents, but they dismissed his fears as an overactive imagination. They assured him that his toys were just toys and couldn't possibly be alive. Determined to prove them wrong, Henry devised a plan to catch his toys in the act.

One night, armed with a flashlight and his courage, Henry hid under his bed, peering out into the room. As the clock struck midnight, a strange energy filled the air, and Henry's toys began to stir. Mr. Chuckles' wooden mouth moved, whispering words Henry couldn't quite make out. The other toys danced and laughed, their once friendly faces twisted into unsettling expressions.

Henry's heart pounded in his chest as he watched in terror, realizing that it wasn't just Mr. Chuckles that was alive, but all of his toys. The room became a frightening playground as they gleefully taunted him, their innocent facades crumbling away to reveal their true nature.

Driven by scared adrenaline, Henry sprung out from beneath the bed, snatching Mr. Chuckles in his trembling hands. He held the dummy tightly, his voice trembling but filled with determination. "Stop! Leave me alone!" he cried out.

To Henry's surprise, the toys froze in their tracks, their mischievous grins replaced with expressions of shock. The room fell silent as Henry's plea resonated through the air. And then, slowly, the toys began to return to their lifeless states, their once animated forms becoming nothing more than inanimate playthings.

Henry realized that it was his belief and refusal to be controlled by fear that had subdued his toys. From that day forward, Henry's toys remained ordinary toys, and Mr. Chuckles was nothing more than a silent companion.

As Henry grew older, he often wondered if the events of that night were just a figment of his imagination. But whenever he saw a ventriloquist dummy or glanced at his old toys, he couldn't shake the feeling that they had once been alive.

THE PAINTING

My grandmother lives in Texas, so I don't get to see her often. My parents sent me to stay with her for the summer. When I got to her house, there was a weird musty smell that hit me right in the face as I walked in the doorway. Her house was ancient looking, like something you would see in a haunted house movie.

As I walked through the house, I noticed she had paintings hung up everywhere. Some were old-looking people dressed in funny uniforms, some were landscapes, and some were creepy-looking creatures. She told me to give her my suitcase, and she would bring it to my room while I washed for supper. It was already 8 p.m. by the time I arrived, and I was starving. We sat in the dining room and mostly ate in silence, with her asking me only a couple of questions about how well I did in school and if I behaved for my parents. Then, she told me a story about her late husband who used to be a lumberjack. How he loved carrying his ax around and got so much pleasure out of chopping trees down. She said he could be seen wandering around outside with his ax on his shoulder even when he wasn't chopping trees. But as he got older, his mind started to go. He had dementia and acted crazy. She said on the day that he passed away, she found him lying there, ax in his hands.

Once we were all done eating, my grandmother said I should get some sleep because she had lots of housework for me to do the next day, and I would need a good night's sleep. I walked down the hall to my room. The house was so dim because my grandmother hardly had any lights on. I got into my room and hopped into bed. My grandmother said, "Goodnight," turned the lights off, and shut the door. For a while, I just lay there, looking around the creepy dark room, with shadows cast everywhere and sounds of creaking that could be heard.

I rolled over and was startled by this super creepy painting hanging on the wall. It's a painting of this angry-looking man holding an ax. His eyes appeared so realistic as if they were staring right down at me in my bed. 'Maybe this is a portrait of my grand-ma's late husband,' I thought to myself. I decided to roll over and not look towards that wall.

In the morning, I was woken up by immense sunlight lighting

up my room. The once-dark room was now brightly lit up. I rolled over to face the wall and was frozen in fear. What I thought was a painting last night was now just a window.

BUNNY

Deep in the heart of a forgotten forest, shrouded in darkness and mystery, lived a creature unlike any other—the flesh-eating bunny. It was said that this abomination of nature was the result of a cruel experiment gone wrong, conducted by a mad scientist who dabbled in forbidden arts.

Legend had it that the bunny had once been an innocent creature, a fluffy and harmless woodland dweller. But through the scientist's sinister designs, it transformed into a monstrous predator, driven by an uncontrollable hunger for human flesh. Its once gentle demeanor had been replaced by a sinister, bloodlust-filled gaze.

News of the flesh-eating bunny spread fear among the villagers who lived on the outskirts of the forest. They told tales of its gruesome attacks, its razor-sharp teeth tearing through flesh with an unholy hunger. No one dared to venture into the forest, for they knew that the bunny lurked within the shadows, waiting for its next victim.

One fateful evening, a group of curious teenagers decided to test their bravery by venturing into the forbidden forest. The allure of uncovering the truth behind the legends was too strong to resist. Armed with flashlights and trembling with anticipation, they entered the dense undergrowth, unaware of the horrors that awaited them.

As they walked deeper into the forest, the air grew heavy with an eerie silence. The usual sounds of wildlife were conspicuously absent, replaced by an unsettling stillness. Branches twisted and gnarled, reaching out like skeletal fingers, and an ominous fog began to seep through the trees.

Suddenly, a rustling sound echoed through the underbrush. The teenagers froze, their hearts pounding in their chests. From the darkness emerged a pair of gleaming red eyes—the flesh-eating bunny had found its prey.

In a flurry of movement, the bunny pounced, its teeth bared and dripping with saliva. The teenagers screamed, their voices drowned out by the creature's blood-curdling shrieks. Its fur, once soft and innocent, was now matted with the blood of its victims.

With a swift and deadly strike, the bunny tore into the flesh of one of the teenagers, leaving behind a gruesome scene of horror.

The others scattered in panic, desperately trying to escape the clutches of the demonic creature.

Through the winding forest, they ran, their terrified screams filling the air. But no matter how fast they ran, the bunny seemed to be everywhere at once—its glowing red eyes appearing in the shadows, its haunting cries echoing through the trees. It was as if the forest itself conspired to keep them trapped in their grisly fate.

In their final moments of desperation, the remaining teenagers stumbled upon an old, dilapidated cabin. With a surge of hope, they rushed inside, slamming the door shut behind them. But the bunny was relentless, relentlessly clawing at the door, its inhuman screeches piercing through the wood.

Inside the cabin, the teenagers huddled together, their breaths ragged and their faces pale with fear. They could feel the bunny's presence, its malevolence seeping through the cracks. But they refused to surrender to their grim fate.

As the flesh-eating bunny relentlessly clawed and scraped at the door of the old cabin, the teenagers huddled together in a state of panic and desperation. Fearful for their lives, they knew they had to act quickly if they were to escape the clutches of the demonic creature.

With hearts pounding and adrenaline coursing through their veins, they spotted an animal trap in the corner of the cabin. An idea formed in their minds—a risky plan to trap the bunny inside the cabin and ensure their own survival.

Acting swiftly, they carefully set up the trap, hoping that it would prove strong enough to hold the monstrous creature at bay. With every creak and scratch from the door, their anxiety escalated, but they were determined to see their plan through.

The bunny, sensing its prey still within reach, intensified its efforts to break through the door. But the teenagers were ready.

With a coordinated effort, they lured the creature towards the trap, guiding it with caution and precision.

As the bunny approached, its malevolence undeterred, it inadvertently triggered the animal trap. The rusty jaws snapped shut, imprisoning the creature within its confines. The teenagers gasped in both relief and terror, as they knew the bunny's insatiable hunger would not be subdued easily.

With the bunny now contained, they quickly shut the door, leaving the cabin in a hurry, praying that no one would ever find it and unknowingly release the demonic creature back into the world.

Going Down

I have been having weird dreams and disturbing thoughts lately. I hear voices in my head that won't go away. It's been upsetting me so much that I can't think or sleep.

Finally, I called a therapist. She was very nice and said, "I promise I will make those thoughts go away." The way she said it, though, sounded eerily strange. She told me to come downtown to the Fountain Plaza building, floor 67, on Tuesday. "What room?" I ask.

"No room number. Just floor 67. You can't miss us when you arrive," she replies.

On Tuesday, I showed up. I looked up at the building, trying to count how many floors I could see. Online, it says there are 83 floors. I walked inside the main lobby and looked for the elevator. I got in and pressed the button for my floor. As the lights showed floor 60, the elevator stopped. A red light turned on. I was stuck in the elevator for about 5 minutes when all of a sudden, the door opened. A man in a red bellhop uniform was standing there and said, "Sorry, sir. We are having difficulties with the elevators at the moment."

I said, "Okay, I can walk the rest of the way, I guess." I only had 7 more floors to walk up. I went into the stairwell and started my ascent.

I reached the door that said, 'floor 67.' I opened it to find myself staring at the roof of the building. I thought to myself, "This can't be. The building has 83 floors, not 67." I closed the door and looked up and down. There were still stairs going up in the stairwell. But where do they go if I am already on the roof? Maybe someone labeled the doors wrong. I walked down the stairs to the next floor. I was halted by the sight of the number on the door. Another 67. I opened this door to find the same rooftop. What is going on? Am I going mad?

I sprinted down what I think were 3 flights of stairs. I grabbed the door and flung it open. The rooftop again! Over and over, no matter how many floors I go up or down, I always end up on the rooftop. Why did the woman tell me to come to the 67th floor? What is happening?

This went on for what seemed like weeks. Trapped on the stair-well with no escape. My body was so exhausted; I could barely move. I opened the door once more. I walked onto the rooftop and went to the edge. I tried yelling down, hoping that someone would finally hear me and save me. It was no use. I was too high up. I was never going to get off this roof.

Staring over the edge of the building down at the street below, an idea popped into my head.

There was another way down.

LAUGHING JACK

One fateful evening, a group of friends, including a brave young boy named Danny, decided to attend the local carnival. Laughter filled the air as they indulged in cotton candy, rode exhilarating roller coasters, and played whimsical games. But the funhouse beckoned to them with an inexplicable allure, its entrance guarded by Laughing Jack, a clown known for his twisted sense of humor and the creepy aura that surrounded him. His presence cast a dark shadow over the fun house, an attraction that unsuspecting visitors would soon come to fear.

As Danny and his friends approached, their curiosity mingled with a sense of unease. Laughing Jack's wide grin seemed to stretch from ear to ear, his eyes glinting with a mischievous spark.

"Step inside my world of fun and fear," Laughing Jack taunted, his voice dripping with wickedness. "Prove your bravery and discover the secrets that lie within the funhouse."

Drawn in by the challenge, Danny and his friends exchanged determined glances. With hesitant steps, they entered the funhouse, unaware of the horrors that awaited them inside.

As the door closed behind them, the air turned heavy, charged with an otherworldly presence. The interior of the funhouse twisted and contorted, defying the laws of reality. The floor seemed to ripple beneath their feet, shifting and bending like an unholy creature. Their hearts raced as they navigated the disorienting maze of distorted mirrors and twisting corridors.

Whispers filled the air, carrying disembodied laughter and eerie tunes that seemed to come from another realm. Figures lurked in the shadows, their elongated limbs reaching out with grasping hands, their faces twisted into grotesque masks. Nightmarish apparitions taunted the friends at every turn, their presence eliciting terror beyond imagination.

Suddenly, everything went pitch black and dead silent. The only thing Danny could hear was his breath. "Guys. Where are you?" Danny said into the void of nothingness. No answers came back. Danny tried to reach out and touch his friends, but his hand felt nothing.

That's when Danny felt the first hand touch his ankle. Then, his other ankle. One by one, hands grabbed Danny, pulling him in different directions. "Stop! Stop! Get me out of here! Danny yelled into the darkness. A second later, the hands stopped, leaving Danny alone again in the dark. Tears started to form in his eyes. Danny reached out once more, hoping to find a wall or something to help guide him out of the funhouse.

As Danny reached to his right and left, he felt a wall on both sides of him. But something weird was happening. The walls were moving closer and closer towards him. Danny attempted to run forward but was met face-to-face with another wall in front of him. Walls on all sides of Danny, closing in on him. Danny was stuck on all sides, unable to move. He pounded and pounded on the wall in front of him screaming, "Help! Help! Someone, help me!" A moment later, Danny could see slightly in front of him as his friends had removed the wall in front of him. Danny stepped forward and looked back to see that he was just trapped in a coffin.

Danny's heart pounded in his chest, his breaths shallow and rapid. He could feel the weight of fear pressing down upon him, threatening to consume him entirely. But he refused to succumb. With every ounce of courage, he led his friends forward, desperate to escape the clutches of the nightmarish funhouse. He pushed his way through doors that seemed to be held shut by a ghostly presence trying to keep it closed.

Finally, the friends burst through the exit, their screams of terror filling the night air. As they stumbled back into the carnival grounds, their relief was short-lived. They turned to gaze upon the funhouse they had just escaped from, only to find a small, gentle kiddie ride in its place.

How could this be? As the boys stood puzzled in a confused fear, they could hear the echoes of evil laughter all around them.

They couldn't see him, but they knew that it was Laughing Jack, taunting them.

As the friends caught their breath and left the carnival, they realized that some nightmares cannot be left behind. The memory of Laughing Jack's malevolence would forever linger in their minds.

MOM

One day, I was in my room playing video games. I hear my mom yelling from down the hall to come into the kitchen to have lunch. I walk out of my room, down the hall, and as I pass by the closet door, someone grabs me and pulls me into the closet. The person quickly covers my mouth so I can't speak. I hear my mom whisper into my ear, "That was not me that called you into the kitchen."

Philip Clark

In the small town of Crestwood, there existed a haunting legend around the tragic fate of a young boy named Philip Clark, who met his untimely demise on the very ice he loved so dearly.

Philip was a talented and passionate hockey player, known for his unwavering dedication and exceptional skills. His dreams were filled with visions of becoming a professional hockey player, soaring across the ice in glory. But fate had a different plan in store for him.

It was a crisp winter evening, and the town's hockey rink was alive with the energy of an intense match. The crowd cheered as Philip's team battled their rivals with fierce determination. But tragedy struck when, in the heat of the game, Philip, going strong into the corner, laid a hard hit onto the opposing player, causing the player's stick to break in two.

The broken stick pierced Philip in the chest, stealing his last breath and extinguishing his dreams in an instant. The collective gasp of the crowd was soon followed by a mournful silence, as the weight of the tragedy settled upon their hearts.

Days turned into weeks, and the shock slowly gave way to grief. But something strange began to occur. Reports surfaced of a figure gliding gracefully across the ice during the darkest hours of the night—the spirit of Philip Clark, forever bound to the rink where his life had been cut short.

Witnesses spoke of a ghostly presence, dressed in a tattered hockey uniform, similar to Philip's. His skates carved patterns upon the ice as he moved with ghostly elegance. Some said they could hear the faint sound of a hockey stick striking a puck, echoing through the empty rink.

The legend of Philip Clark's ghostly appearances spread throughout the town, capturing the imaginations of both young and old. Some believed he was trapped between worlds, reliving the joy he once found in the game that was stolen from him. Others thought his spirit lingered, hoping to inspire future generations of hockey players.

Over time, the sightings of Philip on the ice became a treasured tradition in Crestwood. Children would gather near the rink, bundled up in warm coats and scarves, their eyes fixed on the ghostly figure. They whispered stories of his talent and determination, seeking inspiration in his tragic tale.

As the years passed, the town's love for hockey grew stronger, fueled by the memory of Philip's passion. Each winter, as the rink was prepared for the season, a quiet calmness settled upon the players and spectators. They knew that Philip's spirit would be present, a silent guardian of the game he loved.

And so, the legend of Philip Clark, the boy who died on the ice, lived on. His spirit, forever skating in the realm between the living and the departed, served as a reminder of the fragility of life and the enduring power of pursuing one's dreams. Crestwood would forever cherish his memory, ensuring that his name and his love for the game would never fade away.

FRIDAY NIGHT OUT

It was Friday night, and we decided to have a girls' night out. I left my apartment and met my friends at a restaurant for drinks and sushi. While at the restaurant, I realized my phone was not in my purse. I looked around to see if I had dropped it anywhere. I asked my friend Carly if I could borrow her phone to call mine. I dialed my number and listened as someone picked up. I heard a strange man's voice say, "Hello."

I responded, "Why do you have my phone?" The man on the other end let out a little laugh and hung up. Great! Now someone stole my phone tonight. I went on with my night, trying not to let it ruin everything, as I would have to buy a new one tomorrow.

I got back to my apartment and threw my keys on the kitchen counter, only to notice that my phone was sitting right there. I paused for a while, not knowing what to think. Then I heard a sound coming from my bedroom.

Abigail

Deep in the heart of a small village, nestled between rolling hills, stood an ancient church known as St. Mary's. Its weathered stones and gothic architecture held stories of devotion and faith that spanned generations. But among the tales of piety, there existed a chilling legend—a ghostly presence known as Abigail, the Soul Thief.

Abigail was said to be a tortured soul, trapped within the confines of the church, her spirit forever restless. According to the legends of the townsfolk, she roamed the halls and corridors, her ghostly form draped in tattered garments, her eyes glowing with a hunger for souls.

The legend spoke of a curse that had befallen Abigail centuries ago. Driven by a deep longing for eternal life, she made a pact with dark forces, exchanging her mortal soul for immortality. But her choice came at a terrible cost—forever bound to the church, she was condemned to roam its sacred halls, stealing the souls of those who dared to enter.

It was said that Abigail would appear to unsuspecting visitors, luring them deeper into the church's shadows with promises of enlightenment and salvation. Once entranced by her spectral beauty, she would strike, draining their very essence and leaving them as lifeless husks.

One night, a curious traveler named Samuel arrived in the village. Intrigued by the stories that surrounded St. Mary's, he ventured into the church, determined to uncover the truth behind the haunting legend. Unbeknownst to Samuel, he had entered a realm of darkness and despair.

As he walked through the creaking doors, a chill settled upon him. The air grew thick with a suffocating presence, and the flickering candlelight cast eerie shadows upon the cold stone walls. The silence was deafening, broken only by the distant echoes of his footsteps.

Samuel's heart pounded in his chest as he explored the church's winding corridors. Each step sent shivers down his spine as if unseen eyes watched his every move. He felt a subtle shift in the atmosphere, as though an otherworldly force was drawing him deeper into the church's clutches.

Then, he saw her—a ghostly figure draped in a flowing white gown. Abigail's piercing gaze locked onto Samuel, her eyes gleaming with an unholy hunger. But unlike the others before him, Samuel possessed a resilience, an unwavering spirit that refused to be consumed by fear.

With each encounter, Samuel resisted Abigail's allure, evading her attempts to ensnare his soul. He delved further into the church, unearthing ancient texts, and forgotten relics, seeking a way to break the curse that bound Abigail to her spectral existence.

As Samuel conducted his relentless search, digging through old texts, and sorting through dust-covered scrolls, he discovered an ancient spell—a chant of liberation, believed to hold the key to freeing Abigail's tormented spirit. Armed with newfound knowledge and determination, he returned to the heart of the church, where Abigail awaited.

As Abigail approached, her spectral form exuding a sense of both yearning and desperation, Samuel recited the spell. The air crackled with energy, and the church trembled in response, shaking the very earth that it stood on. Abigail's haunting cries filled the sanctuary as her form began to fade, her eternal entrapment coming to an end.

In a final burst of light, Abigail vanished, her curse broken at last. The church stood in silence, now free from her tormenting presence. Samuel, weary but triumphant, emerged from St. Mary's, the weight of the haunting legend lifted from his shoulders.

From that day forward, the village of St. Mary's knew peace. The legend of Abigail, the Soul Thief, remained etched in their memories—a reminder of the dangers that lie within the shadows, but also the power of courage and determination to conquer even the most malevolent forces that haunt our world.

HELLO DOLLY

Let me start by saying, "I hate dolls."

One day, my mom, sister, and I went to a local store to buy some antique cabinets my mom wanted. My sister and I went our separate ways so that we could each look at the stuff we wanted. My sister announced, "I really hope they have a rocking horse."

As I get towards the back of the store, I notice this super creepy old doll up on a shelf. It has long black hair and painted circles for rosy cheeks. As I walk past it, I swear the eyes are following me. I continued looking at some snow globes I found on a shelf, look back at the doll, and notice the head now looks like it turned and is facing me. I shake it off and turn the corner to look at some other items.

I hear my sister yelling for me, "Come look at this!"

I come back the way I came, and as I am walking, I notice that the doll is now gone. I looked around to see if it had fallen. Nothing. Just gone. I continued towards my sister to find her rocking on a rocking horse. But she was also holding something in her arms. It was the doll. I asked my sister, "Where did you get that?"

She replied, "She was just sitting here on the rocking horse."

I stood there confused. How did the doll get from the shelf and end up on the rocking horse? Did she hear my little sister say she wanted a rocking horse when we came into the store? I figured my sister must have taken the doll down when I wasn't looking.

My mom came over and asked us if we were ready to go. "Do you want to get the rocking horse with your money?" she asked my sister.

"No! I want Dolly! She said she will be my best friend forever if I take her home."

I thought to myself, "What do you mean she said…"

My mom agreed and said, "OK, it's your money."

Later that day, I couldn't stop looking at the creepy doll. It was so evil-looking. Dolly with that blank stare, vacant eyes, and twisted smile. I swear that every time I looked at it, it was in a new position. An arm would move, and a leg that was crossed would be uncrossed. Sometimes it would just move from the couch to the table and move closer to me.

That night while I was asleep, I had such a terrible nightmare about the doll trying to kill me. I woke up screaming. When I opened my eyes, I saw that Dolly was sitting on the bottom of my bed, just staring at me. I let out another scream, and my dad came running in. He laughed it off when I told him about the doll, and he said it was probably just my little sister playing a trick on me.

The next day my mom told us to start going through our old junk in the basement because we had to get rid of some of our old things for Goodwill. After a while of sorting my things, I turn to go upstairs for lunch when I see Dolly sitting there on the top step of the stairs. My heart almost flew out of my chest. I let out a yell towards my sister, "Get this doll out of here before I throw it in the garbage."

My sister ran over and replied, "That's no way to speak to Dolly. I don't get why she even likes you."

"What do you mean, likes me?" I said.

My sister responds, "Dolly told me that she likes playing with you."

My whole body is now wrapped in fear. I am horrified at this point. "Was Dolly really telling my sister these things?" I snap out of it and storm past my sister and up to my room.

Later that night, I had another nightmare. This time, Dolly is trying to suffocate me with a pillow. She has tied me up with the sheets so I can't move. She covers my face with the pillow, and then... I woke up. Inches from my face is Dolly. She is just sitting there smiling at me. I let out a horrified scream. My dad runs into my room again. I told him about my dream and how Dolly was sitting there next to me.

He just shrugged it off and said, "I'll have a talk with your sister about this in the morning."

I had had enough. Dolly needed to go.

The next day, as my mom was loading up the car to take our stuff to Goodwill, I snatched Dolly, put her in one of the boxes, and taped it shut. I helped my mom load the box into the car.

As I sat there waiting with nervous excitement, I watched as my mom came home, hoping that Dolly wasn't discovered and that I would never have to see her again. My sister was looking all over the house for Dolly. She was devastated to lose her. But I couldn't live like that anymore.

As weeks went by, I finally got that dumb doll out of my head. Then, I saw it. As I walked to the end of the driveway to get our mail out of the mailbox, I saw her. Just sitting there in the window across the street, staring at me.

It was Dolly.

MIDNIGHT

A family, seeking a fresh start, moved into a house with hopes of creating cherished memories. As they settled in, they discovered a stray cat, its fur as black as the night sky, lurking in the corners. The family, captivated by its enchanting gaze and affectionate nature, welcomed it with open arms, believing it to be a delightful addition to their lives.

Days turned into weeks, and the bond between the family and the cat deepened. It purred in their laps, curled up by the fire, and provided comfort during the darkest of nights. The children giggled as it seemed to chase invisible phantoms, their laughter echoing through the house. The cat became an irreplaceable member of the family, bringing them joy and solace.

But as time wore on, peculiar occurrences began to unfold. Objects would mysteriously move, their positions shifting when no one was around. Unsettling meows echoed through the house at odd hours, their source remaining unseen. The cat would vanish for hours at a time and then spontaneously appear somewhere in the house, even in rooms where the doors were closed.

Unease settled upon the family as they realized that the cat, though beloved, was different from any they had encountered before. Determined to uncover the truth, they delved into the house's history and asked neighbors about the previous owners and their cat that was left behind, seeking answers to the unsettling phenomena that plagued them.

In their research, they discovered the truth from an elderly woman neighbor down the street—a story of a cat named Midnight, who had met a tragic end within the very walls they now inhabited. The family that once lived in their home abandoned Midnight when they moved out. The feline had perished, trapped and alone, its spirit bound to the house, forever yearning for companionship.

Shrouded in a foreboding atmosphere, the family confronted the chilling realization that the cat they had cherished was, in fact, a vessel for the restless spirit of Midnight. The once-beloved companion had been a phantom all along.

The family's initial shock slowly gave way to a mixture of fear and curiosity. They had grown fond of Midnight, and the thought of letting go seemed more daunting than facing the unknown. The youngest child, brave beyond their years, took a step forward and extended a trembling hand toward the ghostly feline.

Midnight's spooky figure shimmered and wavered as the child's fingers passed through it. A sensation of both cold and warmth spread through their hand, an uncanny sensation that sent goosebumps up the child's arm. The child exchanged a knowing glance with their parents, and an unspoken agreement settled among them.

Despite the spectral existence of their beloved Midnight, the family chose to embrace this extraordinary and otherworldly connection. They decided to coexist with the enigmatic cat, recognizing that even in death, Midnight continued to bring comfort and companionship.

As nights grew darker and the moon cast haunting shadows, Midnight's presence became a comforting constant. The family could feel the soft brush of spectral fur against their skin, a sensation that brought both a sense of wonder and an underlying sense of the supernatural. Midnight's luminous gaze would meet theirs, and a silent understanding would pass between the living and the spectral.

OLD GRISWALD

In the large county of Chudy, amidst its serene landscapes and rolling hills, an eerie reputation lingers - the county is haunted by an inexplicable phenomenon. Children, vibrant and full of life, have been vanishing without a trace, leaving behind a community gripped by fear and a chilling emptiness that even the warmest sun cannot dispel.

On the edge of the county lived a reclusive farmer named Old Griswald. He was known for cultivating the biggest and most exceptional produce in the entire county. Each week, he would bring his magnificent vegetables and fruits to the local market, attracting curious onlookers and eager customers.

The townsfolk marveled at the size and quality of Old Griswald's crops, but nobody could fathom how he managed to grow such extraordinary produce. Whispers of mystery and suspicion shrouded the farmer, for he kept his farming techniques closely guarded. Some said he must have a secret potion, while others believed he had made a pact with the supernatural.

Jacob and Amelia, two adventurous teenagers with a taste for mysteries, became intrigued by the mysterious farmer and his astonishing crops. They both were raised on farms and could never understand how Old Griswald's crops were always the biggest. They couldn't resist the allure of discovering Old Griswald's hidden methods. So, one foggy morning, they decided to venture to his remote farm, located at the edge of the dark woods.

As they approached the farm, they were greeted by a peculiar sight: scarecrows adorned with an eerie grin, their straw-filled bodies swaying eerily in the breeze. Amelia's heart skipped a beat, but Jacob reassured her, and they pressed on.

They soon met Old Griswald himself, a gaunt figure with gnarled hands and piercing eyes that seemed to see through their very souls. Politely, they asked if they could tour his farm and witness the secrets behind his exceptional produce. Griswald agreed, but his smile gave the two a sense of unease.

As they roamed the farm, Jacob and Amelia noticed something odd. Small mounds of fresh soil were scattered across the fields. When they asked about it, Griswald brushed off the question, claiming it was just part of his farming process.

With each passing moment, their unease grew. They followed

the strange scent that seemed to permeate the air, leading them to a rundown old barn hidden behind the rows of crops. Entering cautiously, they were met with a haunting sight: gruesome portraits hanging on the walls, depicting children with sorrowful eyes. That's when Amelia spotted the workbench in the corner of the barn. She tapped Jacob to bring it to his attention without making noise. They both looked in horror as they saw hands, fingers, and limbs on top of the workbench.

Their hearts pounded in terror as they discovered the ghastly truth. Old Griswald's secret fertilizer that fueled the growth of his magnificent crops was none other than the body parts of missing children from nearby villages. He had made dark bargains to gain his farming prowess, sacrificing innocent lives in return for bountiful harvests.

Panicking, Jacob and Amelia tried to flee, but they were caught by the sinister farmer. Old Griswald grinned malevolently, revealing a collection of preserved fingers and toes, a grotesque testament to his horrifying trade.

Old Griswald decided that they had seen too much and were now a threat to his sinister operation. With a wicked glint in his eye, Old Griswald decreed that they would now become part of the 'fertilizer' for his next harvest. Trapped and desperate, the terrified teenagers could do nothing.

In the end, Old Griswald continued to tend his farm, perpetuating his dreadful secret. The townspeople remained oblivious, praising his amazing produce, unaware of the sinister price behind its growth. Jacob and Amelia were never seen again.

And so, the secretive farmer named Old Griswald continued to thrive, forever concealing his dark and horrifying secret, while the innocent children of the nearby villages unknowingly remained at risk of becoming the next sinister harvest for his monstrous crops.

THE BABYSITTER

In a quiet suburban neighborhood, there lived a family with three young children. The parents, eager for a night out, decided to hire a babysitter.

The parents left the house before the babysitter's arrival, entrusting their children's safety to an unfamiliar face. The children anxiously awaited the arrival of their caretaker. As dusk settled and shadows grew long, the doorbell rang, signaling the arrival of the babysitter.

The children hesitantly opened the door, their eyes widening in alarm as they laid eyes on the babysitter. She stood before them, a gaunt figure with sunken eyes and an unnerving smile plastered across her face. Her voice, laced with an eerie calmness, sent shivers down their spines as she repeatedly reassured them, "Don't worry, I won't let anything happen to you."

As the night unfolded, the children found themselves trapped in a nightmare of the babysitter's making. She moved with an unnatural grace, her every gesture steeped in a disconcerting aura. She would suddenly appear behind them, her breath cold against their necks, whispering unsettling things that made their skin crawl. "The voices you hear in the wind are not just whispers. The mirror shows more than your reflection; it shows your other self."

The children didn't know what to say in reply. "They watch you sleep, from the corners of your room…Watch...always watching…", the babysitter said as she disappeared around the corner.

At one point, they swore she went from one room to the next through a wall, and lights would turn off just from her entering a room.

The babysitter's actions grew increasingly unsettling. She rearranged their toys in disturbing patterns to have them facing each other in a circle. Some of them with their eyes fixated on the doorways so that they could see anyone that entered the room. She placed mirrors facing each other, casting eerie reflections throughout the house, and extinguished all the lights, leaving only the flickering glow of a single candle. The children, trembling with fear, began to doubt the babysitter's intentions.

Just as their terror reached its peak, the ringing of a phone shattered the silence. The children rushed to answer, their hands trembling as they held the receiver to their ears. It was their parents on the line, but their voices carried a mix of concern and confusion. They explained that the babysitter had called in sick, and they were on their way home.

A chilling realization struck the children like a bolt of lightning. If the babysitter had not arrived, then who was this terrifying person lurking in their home?

Panic surged through their veins as they turned to face the impostor, frozen in fear, unable to comprehend the depth of the danger they were in. They sat there, frozen, hoping that their parents would come through the door as fast as possible.

OLD MAN

In the small town of Warren, nestled between rolling hills and dense forests, there lived a mysterious person known only as "The Old Man." His appearance was a haunting sight to behold—tattered, dirty clothes clung to his frail frame, and his eyes held a distant, unsettling gaze. He wandered the streets, seemingly disconnected from reality, occasionally letting out bizarre, hoarse shouts that sent shivers down the spines of anyone who crossed his path.

Among those who were curious about the old man were two adventurous boys named Ethan and Nolan. They were inseparable friends, always seeking excitement and thrills in their quiet little town. They had heard the unsettling tales about the old man but were drawn to the enigma surrounding him. Nolan recounted his favorite tale of the old man—he was spotted wandering inside the home of the wealthiest man in town, Roger Penstein. He was so scared, he ran out of his house in his underwear. When the cops arrived, they didn't find anyone.

One gloomy evening, as they loitered near the town square, they spotted the old man shuffling along the cobbled streets. The setting sun cast an eerie glow on his haggard face, making him appear like a specter from a ghostly tale. A group of girls exiting the movie theater stumbled upon him, and he let out an abrupt, chilling cry that sent them fleeing in fear.

Intrigued and disturbed, Ethan and Nolan decided to unravel the secrets of the old man. They decided to follow him discreetly as he left the town square that very night. The old man wandered slowly up the country road, and the boys stealthily kept their distance, hiding behind trees and bushes.

As they ventured deeper into the woods, their fear grew. The trees seemed to whisper ominous warnings, and the darkness enveloped them like a shroud. Yet, their determination to discover the truth urged them forward.

Finally, they witnessed a sight that would haunt their nightmares forever. The old man reached a secluded part of the forest, where an ancient, weathered tombstone lay half-buried under the overgrown foliage. He knelt before the grave. Ethan and Nolan watched in horror as the old man lowered himself into the open grave, disappearing into the ground like a ghostly apparition. They couldn't believe their eyes; the realization that the old man was a ghost that haunted the town.

Terrified and panic-stricken, the boys turned and ran as fast as they could, their hearts pounding in their chests. The woods seemed to echo with the old man's haunting cries, and they couldn't shake the feeling that he was chasing them.

Back in town, they gasped for breath, their faces pale with terror. They swore to never speak of what they had seen to anyone, fearing that no one would believe their terrifying encounter.

From that night on, they couldn't lose the feeling of being watched, of being followed by the old man's tormented spirit. The town of Warren remained shrouded in an eerie, haunting silence, and the legend of the old man and his unsettling walks would continue to haunt the town's residents for generations to come.

THE BASEMENT

Once there was a family that held regular gatherings at Grandma Anna's house. It was a tradition that brought everyone together, filling the old house with laughter, delicious food, and cherished memories. However, there was something eerie that lurked beneath the surface of these joyful occasions.

At each gathering, Uncle Pat, Chris, and Kyle had a

mischievous tradition of giving scary basement tours to the younger kids. The basement was a dimly lit, musty place with creaky wooden stairs that led to mysterious depths. Pat, known for his love of pranks, always took the lead in orchestrating the scares.

As the children eagerly gathered around, Pat would begin the tour by telling made-up stories about old legends that supposedly took place in the basement. "In this very basement, over 100 years ago, an old woman, a very well-known musician, passed away. If you listen closely, you can hear the sounds of her playing the piano." Pat would then hit the play button on a piano recording hidden inside his pocket so the children could hear the faint sound of a piano playing.

He spun tales of ghostly apparitions, previous homeowners, hidden treasures, and haunted artifacts, filling the minds of the young ones with a mix of curiosity and apprehension.

Meanwhile, Chris and Kyle would quietly slink away, disappearing into the back room or hiding behind the old furnace. They waited patiently, relishing in the anticipation of scaring their unsuspecting cousins. They whispered to one another, plotting their next move.

Just as the children reached the climax of the stories, their hearts racing with fear, a sudden noise would echo through the basement. Chris and Kyle, hidden in the shadows, expertly played their part, creating spine-chilling sounds that echoed off the walls. The children jumped, their eyes widening with terror as they clung to one another.

But Uncle Pat wasn't done with his frightful surprises. He had an old doll of Grandma Anna's, a creepy relic from her childhood, that he would secretly place in the laundry chute. With perfect timing, the doll would topple down, its eerie eyes seemingly following the children's every move. Their screams filled the air, and even the adults couldn't help but shudder at the unexpected sight.

As the years went by, the children grew older, and the family gatherings continued. However, a strange phenomenon began to unfold. The stories told by Uncle Pat started to become more vivid as if they were no longer purely works of fiction. The legends he once invented seemed to take on a life of their own, as though the basement had absorbed them, turning them into something tangible.

People would often hear the loud banging on the furnace and ghostly noises coming from the basement when everyone was present in the dining room. The doll that Pat once used to scare the children was now being found throughout the house as if it wandered on its own. The sound of a piano could be heard from the basement even though there was no piano down there.

Despite the growing unease, the family persisted in gathering at Grandma Anna's house. They couldn't resist the allure of tradition and the warmth that enveloped them when they were together. But as they exchanged glances across the dinner table, they couldn't help but wonder if there was more to Uncle Pat's stories than they had ever imagined.

And so, the family gatherings continued, each one tinged with an underlying sense of fear and curiosity. Whether it was the influence of the basement's mysteries or the product of vivid imaginations, no one could say for certain. But one thing was clear – every time they stepped foot into Grandma Anna's house, they couldn't help but wonder what awaited them in the shadows of the basement.

APPARITION

In a quiet, forgotten town, a chilling legend has circulated for decades, recounting the appearance of a spectral being known as "The Apparition." With the image of a bearded ghost, a floating creature with only a head, this ghostly manifestation is said to haunt those who stumble upon its presence.

Sarah, a curious and adventurous teenager, stumbles upon an old photograph while exploring her family's attic. The photo captures a group of townspeople gathered around an eerie figure—The Apparition. Intrigued by the image, Sarah embarks on a quest to uncover the truth behind the ghostly legend.

Driven by her desire for answers, Sarah delves into the town's forgotten history, scouring dusty archives at the local library and interviewing elderly residents. The more she uncovers, the more unsettling the truth becomes. The Apparition was once a respected physician named Dr. Nathaniel Cross, whose experiments in the pursuit of eternal life led to his untimely demise and subsequent transformation into the malevolent apparition.

As Sarah digs deeper, she starts experiencing strange occurrences—whispers in the wind, cold drafts, and the sensation of being watched. The townspeople grow increasingly wary, convinced that Sarah's meddling has awakened the vengeful spirit.

Haunted by nightmares and plagued by apparitions, Sarah's determination wavers. However, she discovers an old diary that belonged to Dr. Cross himself, revealing his descent into madness and the dark secrets he tried to unlock.

Diary Entry – September 7th

I've been digging deep into these ancient books, searching for the secret to living forever. It's like chasing a hidden treasure, something nobody's ever found. My mind's tangled up in these strange words, trying to understand the magic hidden within them.

But things have been getting weird lately. Dreams that feel too real, like they're bleeding into my waking hours. Shadows dance and whisper, and sometimes I talk back, like they're my new friends. My thoughts are slipping, like sand through my fingers, and I can't quite hold on.

I keep pushing, mixing potions, and saying incantations, all to keep a grip on life. But it's like my grip's loosening. My body's changing, feeling lighter, less solid. I see glimpses of myself in mirrors, but I'm not all there, like I'm fading away.

I thought finding the answers would make things clearer, but it's doing the opposite. The closer I get, the further I feel from what's real. These books are like a map leading me into madness. I'm not just searching for eternal life; I'm losing pieces of myself along the way. It's like my mind's breaking apart, and I'm becoming something else, something between the living and the unknown.

Convinced that understanding The Apparition's tragic past is the key to setting it free, Sarah resolves to confront The Apparition head-on.

On a moonlit night, Sarah ventures to the crumbling remains of Dr. Cross's laboratory, the place where he conducted his ill-fated experiments. Shelves covered in cobwebs, lined with dusty, mismatched glassware, and jars filled with unidentified specimens. A pungent scent of chemicals and decay permeated the suffocating atmosphere, making it abundantly clear that this was a place where unsettling and mysterious science had once thrived. Armed with the knowledge from the diary, she pieces together the steps he took, hoping to unravel the spirit's tormented existence.

Sarah begins to perform the ritual in the laboratory. In the center of the room, Sarah placed an old, weathered book, its pages filled with cryptic symbols and incantations. Her hands trembled as she held a vial of moonlit water, collected on a night when the barrier between realms was said to be thin. With cautious determination, she drew a circle on the floor using a mix of salt and ash, a boundary meant to protect her from the unknown.

Taking a deep breath, Sarah began to recite the ancient verses written in the book. Her voice quivered with a blend of curiosity and trepidation, the words resonating with the energies she sought to harness. As she spoke, the room seemed to respond, its atmosphere growing heavy with anticipation.

With the final incantation, Sarah placed the vial of moonlit water at the center of the circle and stepped back. The air grew charged, and a cool breeze brushed against her skin, carrying a hint of something otherworldly.

Calling upon the spirit of Dr. Cross, The Apparition materialized before her. The creature's mournful wails fill the air, echoing through the dilapidated walls.

Sarah, her voice shaking, addressed the spectral figure before her, "Dr. Cross, I can feel your pain, your anguish. Please, you must find a way to let go."

The Apparition's mournful wails seemed to intensify, its ghostly form flickering as if it held on to some unrelenting torment.

"Tell me," Sarah implored, her eyes locked onto the ethereal presence, "why are you trapped in this eternal agony? What binds you to this place?"

As the room trembled with the echoes of The Apparition's cries, a voice, almost like a distant whisper, emanated from the spectral figure. "Guilt," it murmured, the word laden with sorrow.

Sarah leaned closer, her heart heavy with compassion. "Guilt? What do you mean?"

The Apparition began to manifest more clearly, revealing the anguished features of Dr. Cross. "I sought immortality," it confessed, "to heal my ailing daughter, but my ambition led to tragedy. I tampered with forces beyond my understanding, and in doing so, I unleashed horrors upon this town."

Sarah's eyes welled with tears as she realized the depth of the tragedy that had ensnared Dr. Cross's spirit. "I'm so sorry for what you've endured, Dr. Cross. But now, it's time to find peace, for your sake and the sake of the innocent souls affected by your actions."

The room seemed to hold its breath as Dr. Cross's tortured spirit wavered, torn between the agony of the past and the hope of release.

Realizing that forgiveness is the only path to freedom, Sarah extends her compassion to the tortured spirit, offering solace and absolution for its past misdeeds. With tears streaming down its ethereal face, The Apparition releases a final, sorrowful cry before dissipating into the night.

In the aftermath, the town breathes a collective sigh of relief as the ghostly presence fades. Sarah's bravery and understanding have restored harmony, and the once-forgotten town begins to heal from its haunted past. The photograph that originally captured The Apparition mysteriously disappears, leaving no trace of the ghostly legend.

Sarah, forever changed by her encounter, carries the memory of The Apparition with her, a reminder of the power of empathy and the importance of confronting the darkest parts of ourselves to find redemption and closure.

LITTLE NUN

Nestled in a secluded countryside, stood the ancient Saint Agnes Orphanage. It was said to have been run by a devout order of nuns, known for their strict discipline and unwavering faith. The orphanage's halls were filled with stories of the paranormal, but one tale, in particular, haunted those who dared to speak of it—the legend of the little girl nun.

According to the chilling folklore, a young girl named Kayleigh had been left on the orphanage's doorstep, abandoned by her family. The nuns, in their robes of black and white, took her in and raised her within the convent's walls. Kayleigh was known for her pure-hearted nature and her devout commitment to her faith.

However, tragedy struck when an outbreak of a devastating illness swept through the orphanage. Kayleigh, like so many others, fell victim to the merciless disease. Her passing left the nuns devastated, but it was said that her spirit remained trapped within the convent, forever wandering the halls she once called home.

Years later, a young woman named Ellen arrived at Saint Agnes Orphanage to document its history for her university thesis. Intrigued by the tales of the little girl nun, Ellen felt drawn to uncover the truth behind the haunting legends.

As Ellen delved deeper into her research, she began experiencing peculiar occurrences. Whispers echoed through the hallways as if carried by an unseen presence. Doors creaked open and shut on their own, and a cold breeze seemed to follow Ellen's every step.

One moonlit night, while exploring the abandoned wing of the orphanage, Ellen stumbled upon a forgotten diary hidden beneath the dusty floorboards. The diary belonged to one of the nuns who had lived during Kayleigh's time. Its pages were filled with tales of sorrow, mentioning strange rituals performed by the nuns to summon and communicate with the spirit of the departed Kayleigh.

Driven by curiosity, Ellen decided to recreate one of the rituals described in the diary, hoping to make contact with Kayleigh's ghost. Following the instructions meticulously, she lit candles, chanted spells, and waited in the dimly lit room.

As the clock struck midnight, a presence filled the air—a cold, eerie energy. Ellen's heart raced as a figure materialized before her —a spectral form clad in the tattered robes of a little girl nun.

Kayleigh's face was pale, her eyes hollow, and her presence exuded an otherworldly sorrow.

The atmosphere turned ominous, and Ellen soon realized she had unleashed a force beyond her understanding. The once-innocent spirit had become twisted and vengeful after years of longing for freedom. Kayleigh's ghostly apparition lunged at Ellen, screaming in anguish and torment.

In a desperate struggle to survive, Ellen fought against the ghostly onslaught. She searched for a way to soothe Kayleigh's restless soul, to free her from the anger and despair that had consumed her.

Through tears and murmurs, Ellen pleaded with the little girl nun, reminding her of the love and compassion that had once thrived within the orphanage's walls. With each heartfelt plea, Kayleigh's anger subsided, and a glimmer of recognition shone in her ghostly eyes.

In a final act of forgiveness and redemption, Ellen realized that there was only one way to free Kayleigh's tormented spirit from its endless cycle of despair. As she looked into the ethereal eyes of the little girl nun, her heart stirred with a profound empathy for the suffering that had kept Kayleigh bound to the orphanage all these years.

Ellen understood that Kayleigh's ghostly presence yearned for release, for a chance to find peace beyond the confines of the orphanage's walls. She recognized that the anger and sorrow that shackled Kayleigh's spirit needed a vessel, a willing soul who would shoulder the burden and offer a path to the tranquility she had been denied in life.

With unwavering resolve, Ellen made the heartrending decision to become that vessel. She stepped forward, her outstretched hands reaching toward the wavering figure before her. In the quiet chamber of the orphanage, amidst the remnants of memories long past, Ellen allowed Kayleigh's spirit to merge with her own, the ethereal and the earthly intertwining in a delicate dance.

As Kayleigh's spirit melded with Ellen's, a surge of emotions coursed through her – the sadness, the anger, the longing. Ellen, now a beacon of compassion and selflessness, embraced the weight of Kayleigh's pain, understanding that in doing so, she offered a chance for the little girl's eternal rest. She became a vessel for Kayleigh's anguish, a conduit for the feelings that had held her captive, and hoped to guide her toward the peace that had eluded her for so long.

As Ellen's life force faded away, Kayleigh's spirit dissipated, taking with it the haunting presence that had plagued the orphanage for years. The legends of the little girl nun ceased to be spoken through the halls, and Saint Agnes Orphanage regained a sense of peace.

Ellen's sacrifice was not forgotten. Her story became a reminder of the dangers of meddling with forces beyond comprehension. And in the hearts of those who knew her, she was forever celebrated as a courageous soul who, in her pursuit of truth, found redemption both for herself and for the tormented spirit of the little girl nun.

THE HOLLOW SISTERS

In the heart of a desolate town shrouded in mist, a legend whispered through generations - the tale of "The Hollow Sisters." Three sisters, Harper, Reese, and Quinn, once lived peacefully on the outskirts of the town. However, their solitude led to suspicion and rumors, causing fear to creep into the hearts of the townspeople.

One fateful night, a raging storm tore through the town,

unleashing torrents of rain and lightning. The sisters' cottage stood tall amidst the storm, its eerie silhouette casting an unsettling shadow on the landscape. As the storm raged, a mob of terrified villagers, consumed by paranoia, marched towards the sisters' home, believing them to be witches responsible for the calamities that had befallen their town.

With a fury fueled by irrational fear, the mob surrounded the cottage, demanding justice for their perceived sins. The sisters, aware of the impending danger, tried to reason with the crowd, pleading their innocence, but their words fell upon deaf ears.

In an act of desperation, the eldest sister, Harper, raised her hands, praying to the heavens to shield her siblings and herself. But the townspeople perceived this as a confirmation of their suspicions. A cry of hysteria rang through the air as someone hurled a flaming torch towards the cottage.

The flames engulfed the wooden structure, sealing the sisters' fate. As the fire raged, the three sisters perished inside their home, their haunting wails mingling with the roar of the inferno.

In the aftermath, the town descended into a suffocating silence, haunted by guilt and regret for their brutal act. But even as the flames died down, the sisters' spirits lingered, consumed by the seething anger and bitterness of their wrongful demise.

From that day forth, the town was cursed by The Hollow Sisters' vengeful spirits. One by one, townspeople began to vanish mysteriously, leaving no trace of their existence behind. Fear gripped the remaining residents as they realized that The Hollow Sisters had returned to exact their revenge.

Attempts were made to ward off the vengeful spirits, with brave souls venturing into the sisters' abandoned cottage, armed with crosses, talismans, and ancient incantations. But all efforts were futile. The Hollow Sisters' wrath remained undeterred, and those who dared to challenge them disappeared like shadows in the night.

As the years passed, the town's population dwindled, and dark-ness descended upon the land. The Hollow Sisters' eerie laughter could be heard on moonless nights, echoing through the empty streets. It became a ghost town, trapped in perpetual fear and despair, forever tormented by the wrath of The Hollow Sisters.

Whispers spread beyond the town's borders, warning travelers to steer clear of the cursed place. Tales of The Hollow Sisters became a cautionary legend, a grim reminder that anger and hatred could leave scars on a place that lasts for eternity.

And so, the Hollow Sisters continue to haunt the town forever, their anger never quelled, their thirst for vengeance unrelenting. The once-thriving community now stands as a grim testament to the consequences of a tragic mistake, forever locked in the grasp of The Hollow Sisters' malevolent spirits, waiting in the shadows for their next victim to disappear into oblivion.

Inspiration

The Witch - Inspired by the comment by username Epicaricantic on the post "What is the scariest short story you've ever read?" - https://www.reddit.com/r/AskReddit/comments/1g79if/what_is_the_scariest_short_story_youve_ever_read/

Man at the Window - The idea for this story is based on a legend known as "Killer in the backseat", first written by Carlos Drake in 1968.

Want to Go for a Hike - Inspired by the short story "Solo Camping Trip" by username GorgeouslyMae - https://www.wattpad.com/60573518-short-horror-stories-solo-camping-trip

When You're Alone - Inspired by the comment by username Supportive-kinda on the post "What is the scariest short story you've ever read?" - https://www.reddit.com/r/AskReddit/comments/1g79if/what_is_the_scariest_short_story_youve_ever_read/

House Sitting - Inspired by the Urban Legend "The Clown Statue" - https://www.scaryforkids.com/clown-statue/

First Time - Based on the quote by Emo Philips

The Painting - A retelling of the classic tale of The Portraits (a.k.a. The Cabin in the Woods) by Anonymous, 2009 https://www.creepypasta.com/the-portraits/

Going Down - Inspired by "They got the definition wrong" by username Lloiu - https://www.wattpad.com/374682759-horror-stories-they-got-the-definition-wrong%27-by

Laughing Jack - This was inspired by The Fun House Of Fear episode of SPINE-CHILLING STORIES

Mom - Retelling of the story "That Wasn't Me" by username guwopalyssa - https://www.wattpad.com/amp/152647358

Philip Clark – Inspired by a story told at a local haunted hayride when I was a kid.

Friday Night Out - Inspired by the short scary story "So I lost my phone..." by username Lynxx 10 - https://www.reddit.com/r/shortscarystories/comments/1fjycs/so_i_lost_my_phone/

The Babysitter - This was inspired by The Babysitter from the Beyond episode of SPINE-CHILLING STORIES

ORIGINALS

These story ideas were created by the author and his son, Christian.

Camping
The Bus
The Grinner
My New Friend
The Schoolyard
The Whining Pit
The Red Light
Roommate
Emily
Have You Ever
Toys Will Be Toys
Bunny
Abigail
Hello Dolly
Midnight
Old Griswald
Old Man
The Basement
Apparition
Little Nun
The Hollow Sisters